MICHEL LORIO'S CROSS

MICHEL LORIO'S CROSS

BY

HESBA STRETTON

PUBLISHED BY

CURIOSMITH

MINNEAPOLIS
2010

Published by Curiosmith.
P. O. Box 390293, Minneapolis, Minnesota, 55439.
Internet: curiosmith.com.
E-mail: shopkeeper@curiosmith.com.

ISBN 9781935626114

CONTENTS

MICHEL LORIO'S CROSS

BY HESBA STRETTON

IN the southwest point of Normandy, separated from Brittany only by a narrow and straight river, like the formal canals of Holland, stands the curious granite rock which is called the Mont St. Michel. It is an isolated peak, rising abruptly out of a vast plain of sand, to the height of nearly four hundred feet, and so precipitous towards the west that scarcely a root of grass finds soil enough in its weather-beaten clefts. At the very summit is built that wonderful church, the rich architecture and flying buttresses of which strike the eye leagues and leagues away, either on the sea or the mainland. Below the church, and supporting it by solid masonry, is a vast pile formerly a fortress, castle and prison; with caverns and dungeons hewn out of the living rock, and vaulted halls and solemn crypts; all desolate and solitary now, except when a party of pilgrims or tourists pass through them, ushered by a guide. Still lower down the rock, along its eastern and southern face, there winds a dark and narrow street, with odd antique houses on either side. The only conveyance that can pass along it is the water-cart which supplies the town with fresh water from the mainland. The whole place is guarded by a strong and high rampart, with bastions and battlemented walls; and the only entrance is through three gateways, one immediately behind the other, with a small court between. The second of these strong gateways is protected by two old cannon, taken from the English in 1423, and still pointed out to visitors with inextinguishable pride by the natives of Mont St. Michel.

A great plain of sand stretches around the Mont for miles every way; of sand or sea, for the water covers it at flood-tides, beating up against the foot of the granite rocks and the granite walls of the ramparts. But at neap-tides and *eaux mortes*, as the French say, there is nothing but a desert of brown bare sand, with ripple-marks lying across it, and with shallow, ankle-deep pools of salt water here and there. Afar off on the western sky-line a silver fringe of foam, glistening in the sunshine, marks the distant boundary to which the sea has retreated. On every other side of the horizon rises a belt of low cliffs, bending into a semi-circle, with sweeping outlines of curves miles in length, drawn distinctly against the clear sky.

The only way to approach the Mont is across the sands. Each time the tide recedes a fresh track must be made, like the track along snowy roads; and every traveller, whether on foot or in carriage, must direct his steps by this scarcely beaten path. Now and then he passes a high, strong post, placed where there is any dangerous spot upon the plain, for there are perilous quicksands, imperceptible to any eye, lurking in sullen and patient treachery for any unwary footstep. The river itself, which creeps sluggishly in a straight black line across the brown desert, has its banks marked out by rows of these high stakes, with a bush of leafless twigs at the top of each. A dreary, desolate, and barren scene it is, with no life in it except the isolated human life upon the Mont.

This little family of human beings, separated from the great tide of life like one of the shallow pools which the ebbing sea has left upon its sands, numbers scarcely a hundred and a half. The men are fishers, for there is no other occupation to be followed on the sterile rock. Every day also the level sweep of sands is wandered over by the women and children, who seek for cockles in the little pools; the babble of whose voices echoes far through the quiet air, and whose shadows fall long and unbroken on the brown wilderness. Now and then the black-robed figure of a priest, or of one of the brothers dwelling in the monument on the top of the rock, may be seen slowly pacing along the same dead level, and skirting the quicksands where the warning-posts are erected. In the summer months bands of pilgrims are also to be seen marching in a long file like travellers across the desert; but in winter these visits cease almost wholly, and the inhabitants of the Mont are left to themselves.

Having so little intercourse with the outer world, and living on a rock singled out by supernatural visitants, the people remain more superstitious than even the superstitious Germans and Bretons, who are their neighbours. Few of them can read or write. The new thoughts, opinions, and creeds of the present century do not reach them. They are contented with the old faith, bound up for them in the history of their patron, the archangel St. Michel, and with the minute interest taken in every native of the rock. Each person knows the history of every other inhabitant, but knows little else.

From Pontorson to the Mont the road lies along the old bay of St. Michel, with low hedgerows of feathery tamarind trees on each side as far as the beach. It is not at all a solitary road, for hundreds of long heavy carts, resembling artillery wagons, encumber it, loaded with a grey shaly deposit dug out of the bay. A busy scene of men and women digging in the heavy sand, while the shaggy horses stand by, hanging their heads patiently under the blue-stained sheepskins about their necks.

Two or three persons are at work at every cart; one of them, often a woman, standing on the rising pile, and beating it flat with a spade, while a cheerful clatter of voices is heard on every hand.

But at one time a man might have been seen there working alone, quite alone. Even a space was left about him, as if an invisible circle were drawn, within which no person would venture. If a word were flung at him across this imaginary cordon, it was nothing but a taunt or a curse, and it was invariably spoken by a man. No woman so much as glanced at him. He toiled on doggedly, and in silence, with a weary-looking face, until his task was ended, and the wagon driven off by the owner, who had employed him at a lower rate than his comrades. Then he would throw his blue blouse over his shoulders, and tramp away with heavy tread along the faintly marked trail leading across the beach to Mont St. Michel.

Neither was there any voice to greet him as he gained the gateway, where the men of the Mont congregated, as they always congregate about the entrance to a walled town. Rather, the scornful silence which had surrounded him at his work was here deepened into a personal hatred. Within the gate the women, who were chattering over their nets of cockles, shrank away from him, or broke into a contemptuous laugh. Along the narrow street the children fled at the sight of him, and hid behind their mothers, from whose protection they could shout after him. If the curé met him, he would turn aside into the first house rather than come in contact with him. He was under a ban which no one dared to defy.

The only voice that spoke to him was the
fretful, querulous voice of an old, bedridden
woman, as he lifted the latch, and opened the
door of a poor house upon the ramparts, which
had no entrance into the street; and where he
lived alone with his mother, cut off from all ac-
cidental intercourse with his neighbours.

"Michel! Michel! how late thou art!" she exclaimed; "if thou hadst been a good son thou
wouldst have returned before the hour it is."

"I returned as soon as my work was finished,"
he answered in a patient voice, "I have not lost a
minute by the way."

"Bah! because no one will ask thee to turn in
with them anywhere!" she continued. "If thou
wert like everybody else thou wouldst have
many a friend to pass thy time with. It is hard
for me, thy mother, to have brought thee into
the world, that all the world should despise and
hate thee, as they do this day. Monsieur le curé
says there is no hope for thee if thou art so ob-
stinate; thou must go to hell, though I named
thee after our great archangel St. Michel, and
brought thee up as a good Christian. *Quel mal-
heur!* How hard it is for me to lie in bed all day,
and think of my son in the flames of hell!"

Very quietly, as if he had heard such com-
plainings hundreds of times before, did Michel
set about kindling a few sticks upon the open
hearth. This was so common a welcome home
that he scarcely heard it, and had ceased to heed
it. The room, as the flickering light fell upon it,

was one of the cheerless and comfortless chambers to be seen in any peasant's house. A pile of wood in one corner, a single table with a chair or two, a shelf with a few pieces of brown crockery, and the bed on which the paralytic woman was lying, her hands crossed over her breast, and her bright black eyes glistening in the gloom. Michel brought her the soup he had made, and fed her carefully and tenderly, before thinking of satisfying his own hunger.

"It is of no good, Michel," she said, when he laid her down again upon the pillow he had made smooth for her, "It is of no good. Thou mayst as well leave me to perish, it will not weigh for thee. Monsieur le curé says if thou hadst been born a heretic, perhaps the good God might have taken it into account. But thou wert born a Christian, as good a Christian as all the world, and thou hast sold thy birthright to the devil. Leave me then, and take thy pleasure in this life, for thou wilt have nothing but misery in the next."

"I will not leave thee,—never!" he answered, briefly. "I have no fear of the next world."

He was a man of few words evidently. Perhaps the silence maintained around him had partly frozen his power of speech. Even to his mother he spoke but little, though her complaining went on without ceasing, until he extinguished both fire and lamp, and climbed the rude ladder into the loft overhead, where her voice never failed to rouse him from his sleep,

if she only called "Michel!" He could not clearly explain his position even to himself. He had
gone to Paris many years before, where he came
across some Protestants, who had taught him
to read the Testament, and instructed him in
their religion. The new faith had taken hold of
him, and thrust deep roots into his simple and
constant nature; though he had no words at
command to express the change to others, and
scarcely to himself. So long as he had been in
Paris there had been little need of this.

But now his father's death had compelled
him to return to his native place, and to the little knot of people who knew him as old Pierre
Lorio's son, a fisherman like themselves, with
no more right to read or think than they had.
The fierceness of the persecution he encoun-
tered filled him with dismay, though it had not
shaken his fidelity to his new faith. But often
a dumb, inarticulate longing possessed him to
make known to his old neighbours the reason
of the change in him, but speech failed him. He
could only stammer out his confession, "I am no
longer a Catholic, I am a Protestant. I cannot
pray to the saints; not even to the archangel
St. Michel, or the Blessed Virgin. I pray only
to God." For anything else, for explanation, and
for all argument, he had no more language than
the mute, wistful language one sees in the eyes
of dumb creatures, when they gaze fully at us.

Perhaps there is nothing more pitiful than
the painful want of words to express that which

lies deepest within us. A want common to us all, but greatest in those who have had no training in thus shaping and expressing their inmost thoughts.

There was not much to fear from a man like this. Michel Lorio was a living lesson against apostasy. As he went up and down the street, and in and out of the gate, his loneliness and dejection spoke more eloquently for the old faith than any banishment could have done. Michel was suffered to remain under a ban, not formal and ceremonial, but a tacit ban, which quite as effectively set him apart, and made his life more solitary than if he had been dwelling alone on a desert rock out at sea.

Michel accepted his lot without complaint, and without bitterness. He never passed Monsieur le curé without a salutation. When he went daily for water to the great cistern of the monastery, he was always ready to carry the brimful pails too heavy for the arms of the old women and children. If he had leisure he mounted the long flights of grass-grown steps three or four times for his neighbours, depositing his burden at their doors, without a word of thanks for his help being vouchsafed to him. Now and then he overheard a sneer at his usefulness; and his mother taunted him often for his patience and forbearance. But he went on his way silently with deeper yearning for human love and sympathy than he could make known.

If it had not been that, when he was kneeling

at the rude dormer window of his loft and gazing dreamily across the wide sweep of sand, with the moon shining across it and the solemn stars lighting up the sky, he was at times vaguely conscious of an influence, almost a presence, as of a hand that touched him and a voice that spoke to him, he must have sunk under this intense longing for love and fellowship. Had he been a Catholic still, he would have believed that the archangel St. Michel was near and about to manifest himself as in former times in his splendid shrine upon the Mont. The new faith had not cast out all the old superstitious nature; yet it was this vague spiritual presence which supported him under the crushing and unnatural conditions of his social life. He endured, as seeing one who is invisible.

Yet at other times he could not keep his feet away from the little street where all the life there was might be found. At night he would creep cautiously along the ramparts and descend by a quiet staircase into an angle of the walls, where he could look on unseen upon the gathering of townsfolk in the inn where he had often gone with his father in earlier days. The landlord, Nicolas, was a most bitter enemy now. There was the familiar room filled with bright light from an oil lamp and the brighter flicker of a wood fire, where the landlord's wife was cooking. A deep, low recess in the corner, with a crimson valance stretched across it, held a bed with snow-white pillows, upon one of which rested a child's curly head with eyes fast sealed against the glare of the lamp. At a table close by sat the landlord and three or four of the wealthier men of the Mont busily and seriously eating the omelets and fried fish served to them from the pan over the fire. The copper and brass cooking utensils glittered in the light from the walls where they hung. It was a cheery scene, and Michel would stand in his cold, dark corner, watching it until all was over and the guests ready to depart.

"Thou art Michel *le diable!*" said a childish voice to him one evening, and he felt a small, warm hand laid for an instant upon his own. It was Delphine, Nicolas's eldest girl, a daring child, full of spirit and courage; yet even she shrank back a step or two after touching him, and stood as if ready to take flight.

"I am Michel Lorio," he answered in a quiet, pleasant voice, which won her back to his side. "Why dost thou call me Michel *le diable?*"

"All the world calls thee that," answered Delphine; "thou art a heretic. See! I am a good Christian. I say my ave and paternoster every night; if thou wilt do the same thing, no one will call thee Michel *le diable.*"

"Thou art not afraid of me?" he asked, for the child put her hand again on his.

"No, no! thou art not the real devil!" she said, "and maman has put my name on the register of the Monument; so the great archangel St. Michel will deliver me from all evil. What canst

thou do? Canst thou turn children into cats? or
canst thou walk across the sea without being
drowned? or canst thou stand on the highest
pinnacle of the church, where the golden image
of St. Michel used to be, and cast thyself down
without killing thyself? I will go back with thee
to thy house and see what thou canst do."

"I can do none of these things," answered
Michel, "not one; but thou shalt come home with
me if thou wilt."

"Carry me," she said, "that I may feel how
strong thou art."

He lifted her easily into his arms, for he was
strong and accustomed to bear heavier burdens.
His heart beat fast as the child's hand stole
round his neck, and her soft cheek touched his
own. Delphine had never been upon the ramparts before when the stars were out and the
distant circle of the cliffs hidden by the night,
and several times he was compelled to stop and
answer her eager questions; but she would not
go into the house when they reached the door.

"Carry me back again, Michel," she demand-
ed. "I do not like thy mother. Thou shalt bring
me again along the ramparts tomorrow night.
I will always come to thee, always when I see
thee standing in the dark corner by our house. I
love thee much, Michel *le diable.*"

It was a strange friendship carried on
stealthily. Michel could not put away from himself this one little tie of human love and fellowship. As for Delphine, she was as silent about

her new friend as children often are of things
which affect them deeply. There was a mingling of superstitious feeling in her affection
for Michel—a half dread that gave their secret
meetings a greater charm to the daring spirit
of the child. The evening was a busy time at
the inn, and if Delphine had been missed, but
little wonder and no anxiety would have been
aroused at her absence. The ramparts were de-
serted after dark, and no one guessed that the
two dark figures sauntering to and fro were
Michel and Delphine. When the nights were
too cold they took refuge in a little overhanging
turret projecting from one of the angles of the
massive walls—a darksome niche with nothing
but the sky to be seen through a narrow em-
brasure in the shape of a cross. In these haunts
Michel talked in his simple untaught way of his
thoughts and of his new faith, pouring into the
child's ear what he could never tell to any other.
By day Delphine never seemed to see him; never cast a look towards him as he passed by amid
the undisguised ill-will of the town. She ceased
to speak of him even, with the unconscious and
natural dissimulation by which children screen
themselves from criticism and censure.

The people of the Mont St. Michel are very
poor, and the women and children are compelled
to seek some means of earning money as well
as the men. As long as the summer lasts the
crowds of pilgrims and tourists, flocking to the
wonderful fortress and shrine upon the summit,

bring employment and gain to some portion of
them, but in the winter there is little to do except when the weather is fine enough to search
for shellfish about the sands, and sell them in
the villages of the mainland. As the tide goes
down, bands of women and children follow it
out for miles, taking care to retrace their steps
before the sea rises again. From Michel's cottage on the ramparts the whole plain toward
Avranches was visible, and he could hear the
busy hum of voices coming to his ear from afar
through the quiet air. But on the western side
of the Mont, where the black line of the river
crosses the sands, they are more dangerous;
and in this direction only the more venturesome
seekers go—boys who love any risk, and widows
who are the more anxious to fill their nets, because they have no man to help them in getting
their daily bread.

The early part of the winter is not cold in
Normandy, especially by the sea. As long as the
westerly winds sweep across the Atlantic, the
air is soft though damp, with fine mists hanging
in it, which shine with rainbow tints in the sun-
light. Sometimes Christmas and the New Year
find the air still genial, in spite of the short days
and the long rainy nights. Strong gales may
blow, but so long as they do not come from the
dry east or frosty north there is no real severity
of weather.

It was such a Christmas week that year.
Not one of the women or children had yet been

forced to stay away from the sands on account of the cold. Upon Christmas Eve there was a good day, though a short one, before them, for it was low water about noon, and the high tide would not be in before six. All the daylight would be theirs. It was a chance not to be missed, for as the tides grew later in the day their time for fishing would be cut shorter. Almost every woman and child turned out through the gate, with their nets in their hands. By midday the plain was dotted over by them, and the wintry sun shone pleasantly down, and the quiet rock caught the echo of their voices. Farther away, out of sight and hearing, the men also were busy, Michel among them, casting nets upon the sea. As the low sun went down in the southern sky, the scattered groups came home by twos and threes, anxious to bring in their day's fishing in time for the men to carry them across to the mainland before the Mont should be shut in by the tide.

A busy scene was that in the gateway.

All the town was there; some coming in from the sands, and those who had been left at home with babies or old folks running down from their houses. There was chaffing and bartering; exchanges agreed upon, and commissions innumerable to be entrusted to the men about to set out for Pontorson, the nearest town. Michel Lorio was going to sell his own fish, for who would carry it for him? Yet though he was the first who was ready to start, not a soul charged

him with a single commission. He lingered wist-
fully and loitered just outside the gateway; but
neither man, woman nor child said, "Michel,
bring me what I want from the town."

He was treading slowly down the rough
causeway under the walls of the town, when
a woman's shrill voice startled him. It was not
far from sunset, and the sun was sinking round
and red, behind bank of fog. A thin, grey mist
was creeping up from the sea. The latest band of
stragglers, a cluster of mere children, were running across the sand to the gate. Michel turned
round, and saw Nicolas's wife, a dark, stern-
looking woman, beckoning vehemently to these
children. He paused for a moment to look at his
little Delphine. "Not there!" he said to himself,
and was passing on, when the shrill voice again
caught his attention.

"Where is 'Phine?" called the mother.

What was it the children said? What answer
had they shouted back? Michel stood motionless, as if all strength had failed him suddenly.
The children rushed past him in a troop. He lifted up his eyes, looking fearfully toward the sea
hidden behind the deepening fog. Was it possible that he had heard them say that Delphine
was lost?

"Where is 'Phine?" asked the mother; but
though her voice was lower now, Michel heard
every syllable loudly. It seemed as if he could
have heard a whisper, though the chattering in
the gateway was like the clamor of a fair. The

eldest girl in the little band spoke in a hurried and frightened tone.

"'Phine is so naughty, Madame," she said, "we could not keep her near us. She would go on and on to the sea. We could not wait for her. We heard her calling, but it was so far, we dared not go back. But she cannot be far behind us, for we shouted as we came along. She will be here soon, Madame."

"Mon Dieu!" cried the mother, sinking down on one of the great stones, either rolled up by the tide, or left by the masons who built the ramparts, "call her father to me."

It was Michel Lorio who found Nicolas, his greatest enemy. Nicolas had a number of errands to be done in the town, and he was busy impressing them on the memory of his messenger, who, like every one else, could neither read nor write. When Michel caught his arm in a sharp, fast grip, he turned round with a scowl, and tried, but in vain, to shake off his grasp.

"Come to thy wife," said Michel, dragging him toward the gate, "Delphine, thy little one, is lost on the sands."

The whole crowd heard the words, for Michel's voice was pitched in a high, shrill key, which rang above the clamor and the babel. There was an instant hush, every one listening to Michel, and every eye fastened upon him. Nicolas stared blankly at him, as if unable to understand him, yet growing passive under his sense of bewilderment.

"The children who went out with Delphine this morning are come back," continued Michel, in the same forced tone, "they are come back without her. She is lost on the sands. The night is falling, and there is a fog. I tell you the little one is alone, quite alone, upon the sands; and it will be high water at six o'clock. Delphine is alone and lost upon the sands!"

The momentary hush of the crowd was at an end. The children began crying, and the women calling loudly upon St. Michel and the Holy Virgin. The men gathered about Nicolas and Michel, and went down in a compact group to the causeway beyond the gate. There the lurid sun, shining dimly through the fog, made the most sanguine look grave and shake their heads hopelessly behind the father and mother. The latter sat motionless, looking out with straining eyes to see if Delphine were not coming through the thickening mist.

"Mais que faire! que faire!" cried Nicolas, catching at somebody's shoulder for support, without seeing whose it was. It was Michel's, who had not stirred from his side since he had first clasped his arm. Michel's face was as white as the mother's; but there was a resolute light in his eyes that was not to be seen in hers.

"Nothing can be done," answered one of the oldest men in answer to Nicolas's cry, "nothing, nothing! We do not know where the child is lost. See! there are leagues and leagues of sand; and one might wander miles away from where the

poor little creature is at this instant. The great
archangel St. Michel protect her!"

"I will go," said the mother, lifting herself
up; and, raising her voice, she called loudly with
a cry that rang and echoed against the walls,
"'Phine! 'Phine! my little 'Phine! come back to
thy poor mother!" but there was no answer,
except the sobs and prayers of the women and
children clustering behind her.

"Thou canst not go!" exclaimed Nicolas,
"there are our other little ones to think of, nor
can I leave thee and them. My God! is there then
no one who will go and seek my little Delphine?"

"I will go," answered Michel, standing out
from among the crowd, and facing it with his
white face and resolute eyes; "there is only one
among you all upon the Mont who will miss me.
I leave my mother to your care. There is no time
for me to bid her adieu. If I come back alive,
well! if I perish, that will be well also!"

Even then there was no cordiality of response
in the hearts of his old friends and neighbours.
The superstition and prejudice of long years
could not be broken down in one moment and
by one act of self-sacrifice. They watched Michel
as he laid his full creel down from his shoulders,
and threw across them in its place the strong
square net with which he fished in the ebbing
tide. His silence was no less expressive than
theirs. Without a sound he passed away bare-
footed down the rude causeway. His face, as
the sun shone on it, was set and resolute with a

determination to face the end, whatever the end might be. He might have so trodden the path to Calvary.

He longed to speak to them, to say adieu to them; but he waited in vain for one voice to break the silence. He turned round before he was too far away, and saw them still clustered without the gate. Every one of them known to him from his boyhood, the story of whose lives had been bound up with his own and formed part of his history. They were all there, except his mother, who would soon hear what peril of the sea and peril of the night he was about to face. Tears dimmed his eyes, and made the group grow indistinct, as though the mist had already gathered between him and them. Then he quickened his steps, and the people of the Mont St. Michel lost sight of him behind a great buttress of the ramparts.

But for a time Michel could still see the Mont as he hurried along its base, going westward, where the most treacherous sands lie. His home was on the eastern side, and he could see nothing of it. But the great rock rose up precipitously above him, and the noble architecture upon its highest point glowed with a ruddy tint in the setting light. As he trampled along no sound could be heard but the distant sigh of the sea, and the low, sad sough of the sand as his bare feet trod it. The fog before him was not dense, only a light haze, deceptive and beguiling; for here and there he turned aside, fancying he

could see Delphine, but as he drew nearer to
the spot he discovered nothing but a post driven
into the sand. There was no fear that he should
lose himself upon the bewildering level, for he
knew his way as well as if the sand had been
laid out in well-defined tracks. His dread was
lest he should not find Delphine soon enough to
escape from the tide, which would surely over-
whelm them both.

He scarcely knew how the time sped by, but
the sun had sunk below the horizon, and he had
quite lost the Mont in the fog. The brown sand
and the grey, dank mist were all that he could
see, yet still he plodded on westward, toward
the sea, calling into the growing darkness. At
last he caught the sound of a child's sobs and
crying, which ceased for a moment when he
turned in that direction and shouted, "'Phine!"
Calling to one another, it was not long before
he saw the child wandering forlornly and deso-
lately in the mist. She ran sobbing into his open
arms, and Michel lifted her up and held her to
his heart with a strange rapture.

"It is thou that hast found me," she said,
clinging closely to him. "Carry me back to my
mother. I am safe now, quite safe. Did the archangel St. Michel send thee?"

There was not a moment to be lost; Michel
knew that full well. The moan of the sea was
growing louder every minute, though he could
not see its advancing line. There was no spot
upon the sand that would not be covered before

another hour was gone, and there was barely
time, if enough, to get back to the Mont. He could
not waste time or breath in talking to the child
he held fast in his arms. A pale gleam of moonlight shone through the vapor, but of little use
to him save to throw a ghostly glimmer across
the sands. He strode hurriedly along, breathing
hardly through his teeth and clasping Delphine
so fast that she grew frightened at his silence
and haste.

"Where art thou taking me, Michel *le diable?*" she said, beginning to struggle in his arms.
"Let me down; let me down, I tell thee! Maman
has said I must never look at thee. Thou shalt
not carry me any farther."

There was strength enough in the child and
her vehement struggles to free herself to hinder
Michel in his desperate haste. He was obliged
to stand still for a minute or two to pacify her,
speaking in his quiet, patient voice, which she
knew so well.

"Be tranquil, my little 'Phine," he said. "I
am come to save thee. As the Lord Jesus came
to seek and to save those who are lost, so am I
come to seek thee and carry thee back to thy
mother. It is dark here, my child, and the sea is
rising quickly, quickly. But thou shalt be safe.
Be tranquil, and let me make haste back to the
Mont."

"Did the Lord save thee in this manner?"
asked Delphine, eagerly.

"Yes, He saved me like this," answered

Michel. "He laid down His life for mine. Now thou must let me save thee."

"I will be good and wise," said the child, putting her arms again about his neck, while he strode on, striving if possible to regain the few moments that had been lost. But it was not possible. He knew that before he had gone another kilometre, when through the mist there rose before him the dark, colossal form of the Mont, but too far away still for them both to reach it in safety. Thirty minutes were essential for him to reach the gates with his burden, but in little more than twenty the sea would be dashing round the walls. The tide was yet out of sight and the sands were dry, but it would rush in before many minutes, and the swiftest runner with no weight to carry could not outrun it. Both could not be saved; could either of them? He had foreseen this danger, and provided for it.

"My little 'Phine," he said, "thou wilt not be afraid if I place thee where thou wilt be quite safe from the sea? See, here is my net! I will put thee within it, and hang it on one of these strong stakes, and I will stand below thee. Thou wilt be brave and good. Let us be quick, very quick. It will be like a swing for thee, and thou wilt not be afraid so long as I stand below thee."

Even while he spoke he was busy fastening the corners of his net securely over the stake, hanging it above the reach of the last tide mark. Delphine watched him laughing. It seemed only another pleasant adventure, like wandering with him upon the ramparts, or taking shelter in the turret. The net held her comfortably, and by stooping down she could touch with her outstretched hand the head of Michel. He stood below her, his arms fast locked round the stake, and his face uplifted to her in the faint light.

"'Phine," he said, "thou must not be afraid when the water lies below thee, even if I do not speak. Thou art safe."

"Art thou safe also, Michel?" she asked.

"Yes, I am safe also," he answered; "but I shall be very quiet. I shall not speak to thee. Yes; the Lord Christ is caring for me, as I for thee. He bound Himself to the cross as I bind myself here. This is my cross, Delphine. I understand it better now. He loved us and gave Himself for us. Tell them, tomorrow, what I say to thee. I am as safe as thou art, tranquil and happy."

"We shall not be drowned!" said Delphine, half in confidence and half in dread of the sea, which was surging louder and louder through the darkness.

"Not thou!" he answered cheerily. "But, 'Phine, tell them tomorrow that I shall never more be solitary and sad. I leave thee now, and then I shall be with Christ. I wish I could have spoken to them, but my heart and tongue were heavy. Hark! there is the bell ringing."

The bell which is tolled at night when travellers are crossing the sands, to guide them to the Mont, flung its clear, sharp notes down from the great indistinct rock, looming through the dusk.

"It is like a voice to me, the voice of a friend; but it is too late!" murmured Michel. "Art thou happy, Delphine, my little one? When I cease to speak to thee wilt thou not be afraid? I shall be asleep, perhaps. Say thy paternoster now, for it is growing late with me."

The bell was still tolling, but with a quick, hurried movement, as if those who rang it were fevered with impatience. The roaring of the tide, as it now poured in rapidly over the plain, almost drowned its clang.

"Touch me with thy little hand, touch me quickly!" cried Michel. "Remember to tell them tomorrow that I loved them always, and I would have given myself for them as I do for thee. Adieu, my little 'Phine. Come quickly, Lord Jesus!"

The child told afterwards that the water rose so fast that she dared not look at it, but shut her eyes as it spread, white and shimmering, in the moonlight all around her. She began to repeat her paternoster, but she forgot how the words came. But she heard Michel, in a loud clear voice, saying "Our Father;" only he also seemed to forget the words, for he did not say more than "Forgive our trespasses, as we forgive—." Then he became quite silent, and when she spoke to him, after a long while, he did not answer her. She supposed he had fallen asleep, as he had said, but she could not help crying and calling to him again and again. The sea-gulls flew past her screaming, but there was no sound of any voice to speak to her. In spite of what he had said to her beforehand, she grew frightened, and thought it was because she had been unkind to Michel *le diable* that she was left there alone, with the sea swirling to and fro beneath her.

It was not for more than two or three hours that Delphine hung cradled in Michel's net, for the tide does not lie long round the Mont St. Michel, and flows out again as swiftly as it comes in. The people followed it out, scattering over the sands in the forlorn hope of finding the dead bodies of Michel Lorio and the child, for they had no expectation of meeting with either of them alive. At last two or three of them heard the voice of Delphine, who saw the glimmer of their lanterns upon the sands, and called shrilly and loudly for succor.

They found her swinging safely in the net, untouched by the water. But Michel had sunk down upon his knees, though his arms were still fastened about the stake. His head had fallen forward upon his breast, and his thick, wet hair covered his face. They lifted him without a word spoken. He had saved Delphine's life at the cost of his own.

All the townspeople were down at the gate, waiting for the return of those who had gone out to seek for the dead. The moon had risen above the fog, and shone clearly down upon them. Delphine's mother, with her younger children about her, sat on the stone where she had been sitting when Michel set out on his perilous quest. She and the other women could see a crowd of the men coming back, carrying some burden among them. But as they drew near to the gate, Delphine sprang forward from among them and ran and threw herself into her mother's arms. "A miracle!" cried some voices amid the crowd; a miracle wrought by their patron St. Michel. If Michel Lorio were safe, surely he would become again a good Christian, and return to his ancient faith. But Michel Lorio was dead, and all that could be done for him was to carry his dead body home to his paralytic mother, and lay it upon his bed in the little loft where he had spent so many hours of sorrowful loneliness.

It was a perplexing problem to the simple people. Some said that Michel had been permitted to save the child by a diabolic agency which had failed him when he sought to save himself. Others maintained that it was no other than the great archangel St. Michel who had securely fastened the net upon the stake and so preserved Delphine, while the heretic was left to perish. A few thought secretly, and whispered it in fear, that Michel had done a noble deed, and won heaven thereby. The curé, who came to look upon the calm dead face, opened his lips after long and profound thought:

"If this man had been a Christian," he said, "he would have been a saint and a martyr."

MONT ST. MICHEL TRAVELOGUE

BY HESBA STRETTON

REPRINTED FROM LEISURE HOUR MAGAZINE, 1873.

THE town-clock of St. Servan, in Brittany, has two minute-hands, one set twenty minutes earlier than the other. The earlier time is that of the railway; the later that of the town. Hence it happened that whilst we were leisurely dressing, and taking our *café au lait*, at six o'clock one summer morning, we were startled out of our self-possession by the rattling of the railway-omnibus over the stony street under our window, and by the loud vociferations of every man and woman about our hotel, fully twenty minutes sooner than we had expected. We ran down with our bonnets, mantles, and gloves in our hands, and finished our toilet in the omnibus, with a dozen pair of brown French eyes fastened steadfastly upon us, and found ourselves at the station quite half an hour before the time for the train to start.

It is a warm, sunny morning, early enough to have a little of the dewy freshness of the night still lingering in the air. Through flat fields, bordered by tall poplar trees, runs the railway, with no other object of interest to be seen than the tobacco plants, set in formal rows less pictur- esque than turnip fields. At Dol, where we leave the train to continue our journey by omnibus, we have a specimen of the boasted superiority of the French in organisation. There are four omnibuses to set off, with about thirty passengers to be car- ried in them, and rather more than half an hour is consumed in this difficult manoeuvre, though the conveyances have been waiting in readiness, with their rough horses harnessed, and appar- ently nothing to be done but for the passengers to take their seats. But no, each person must his name entered in an immense book, and must wait until a place is assigned to him, and not one omnibus can start until the list of names has been called out in a loud voice, and answered to, as in a school. Then we are allowed to go on, one after the other, in a string, as though we formed part of a procession or pilgrimage.

A long, quiet drive, certainly as sober as any English omnibus-load of strangers could be, though all besides ourselves are French. The country itself is quiet, and seems asleep; with none of the stir and movement of our more densely populated land. It is very thickly wood- ed, with here and there a little hamlet some distance from the high road, nestling down in a dingle, its thatched roofs so overgrown with moss and house-leek that they can hardly be distinguished from the green banks sloping

down to them. Small homely churches stand
in the midst, with a single bell hanging under
their low pent-roof belfries. Here and there a
lane runs down from the road, lying deep between high hedgerows, and shaded into a green
twilight by the thick branches of the trees inter-
lacing over it, leading, perhaps, to some solitary
dwelling, half farm and half château, removed
even from the slight din and dust of our small
procession passing by twice a day.

The figures that people this lonely country
are few and far between, but striking enough
to fix themselves for ever on our memory. Now
and then we pass a girl tending sheep by the
wayside, with a distaff in her hand, spinning
mechanically as she stares after us. At some of
the cottage doors women are beating out flax,
and in one farmyard we see a group of men and
women threshing corn on a threshing-floor with
flails, which whirl round their heads in dangerous proximity to their next neighbours, but with
wonderful precision. Here are two picturesque
old beggars, a man and woman, with a little
child between them in a white cap and a fringe
of hair about her face; and not far behind them
comes a very aged man, riding slowly along the
sunny road on a donkey, with a long cloak of
striped bed-ticking covering both it and him.
At every turn we are reminded that we are not
in England, even if the clearness of the atmo-
sphere and brightness of the sunshine could
leave us in any doubt.

About ten o'clock we reach Pontorson, and go through the same protracted ceremony as at Dol, in changing our omnibuses for those which are to take us on to Mont St. Michel. But it is market-day, and the odd figures of the Norman and Breton peasants amuse us too well for the time to hang heavily on our hands. The road after we leave Pontorson is the dustiest that can be imagined; the horses' hoofs sink over the fetlocks into loose, light powder at every step, and raise a cloud around us, which hides the omnibus in front and the one in rear of us. All that can be seen are the whitened hedgerows of feathery tamarisks growing on each side and in bloom if one could but discern the blossom, and long, low tumbrils, which we take at first to be artillery waggons, slowly plodding past us, heavily laden with sand from the old bay of Cancale, where the sea has left a deposit which is now valuable as a manure. Hundreds of these waggons are passing to and fro, each with teams of two or three horses, every one of which adds to the blinding clouds of dust which surround us. We are overjoyed when we reach at last the more solid sands, across which, about a mile away, there rises that which we have come so far to see, and have so long wished to see—the granite peak of the Mont St. Michel of Normandy.

As it stands before us now it has no background save the deep blue of the sky. It juts up directly out of a broad, level plain of sand, alone, with a sharp, clear outline of grey showing well against the blue. At the highest point, about five hundred feet above the plain, the pinnacles and buttresses of the church which crown the summit form a delicate, lace-like tracery against the sky, and give to the whole of the cone of granite an appearance of far greater height than it actually possesses. To the right hand of us the beach is encircled by a low, lovely curve of distant hills, the shore of the Bay of Cancale, which clasps the brown desert of sand and its shallow pools of salt water, with a belt of green lands and scattered villages lying in the sunny light of the summer noon.

The path across the sands is marked out only by the track of other wheels which have come this way since the last spring-tide washed over the plain. Here and there tall, bare poles are erected as a sort of guide, or rather as a beacon against the dangerous places, where the quicksands lie. It is neither safe nor pleasant to get off the beaten track. A friend of ours at St. Servan has told us how a carriage she was in began to sink in the treacherous, shifting sand, and though all who were in escaped, and the horses were unharnessed in time, the wheels were so far sucked in that it was impossible to drag out the carriage, and it sank slowly before their eyes. We hear, too, that it has happened sometimes when a vessel has been run ashore it has been swallowed up, and has completely disappeared in the space of a few hours. Fortunately, we have no opportunity of personally proving the truth of these statements, for we reach the mount in perfect safety, without a qualm of fear.

As we draw nearer we find strong fortifications built against the rock, wherever it is not in itself perpendicular and impregnable. Above the ramparts the little town, consisting of fifty or sixty houses, is seen climbing up the rock to the foot of the abbey, where a second cincture of walls and towers has been built for its defence. A rough stone causeway, very steep, leads to a narrow gateway which will admit only one conveyance at a time. Within is a small court, La Cour du Lion, crowded at this moment by all the inhabitants of the mount who are not busy in providing refreshments for our band of tourists and pilgrims. Beyond is a second gateway— possessing as ornaments on either side two rude pieces of cannon taken from the English in 1427, which are still pointed out with inextinguishable pride to every visitor—a second small court, and then a gateway with a portcullis, the arch of which communicates with the ramparts. After passing through these places of defence one enters the street of the town.

But can it be called a street? There are, to begin with, two noisy little inns, the Golden Lion and the Golden Head of St. Michel, opposite to which stands the high wall of the ramparts, with yellow flowers, and moss and ferns growing in every crevice. Beyond these a narrow winding causeway lies between a double-row of houses, with steps here and there cut out of the rock. The inns are in great bustle and confusion today, for the number of pilgrims is large, and the time they have to stay on the mount is extremely limited, less than two hours, during which they must perform their pilgrimage to the shrine, which secures to them a plenary indulgence, by a bull of the present pope, dated Jan. 12, 1866; and they must also eat their dinner, which tempts them by a delicious fragrance as they go by the inn-door. Some prefer to make sure of their dinner, others of their pardon. As for ourselves, we quickly resolve upon staying at least one night in this unique place, and so gain ample time for both dinner and pilgrimage.

The landlady of the Golden Head, a dark-eyed, gipsy-looking woman, shows us a chamber, and recommends it strongly as being under that of a compatriot, an English artist; but its windows are blinded by the ramparts, and open upon the noise and ill-odours of the narrow street below. We insist upon having a room very tranquil; and after some hesitation she finds a bunch of rusty keys, and invites us to follow her up the rock. On each side of the roughly-paved street the houses rise so high as to keep it in perpetual shade; houses half of timber with round Norman arches over the doorways, and deep cellar doors black with shadow. The women who are sitting on their house-steps wear caps bent like a roof, with long flaps turned up on each side of the face; the men are mostly barefoot and bareheaded, and are dressed in cool blue blouses. There is scarcely a sign of any visitors up here, for their route lies along the ramparts, and we are favoured with some marks of curiosity as we follow our landlady up the street.

She fits the key into the lock of a little house, and ushers us into it, leading the way to one very tranquil room. It is not inviting; the furniture is so simple it can scarcely be called furniture; a candle is stuck upon the chimney-piece with no kind of candlestick to hold it, and there is a good deal of dust lying about. But there are two windows opening straight upon the great plain of brown sand, leagues across, the pure air of the sea blowing over it, with neither smoke nor breath of a town mingling with it; there is perfect silence, except for the quiet rustling of some poplar trees growing under the walls of the abbey above us; and there is perfect freedom, for madame informs us we may keep the key of the house, and carry it in our pockets. We declare ourselves content, and madame, who has been inly afraid of our going over to the Golden Lion, is in raptures, and promises to arrange the room for us immediately. There is a second door, she tells us, opening upon the ramparts.

This gives the finishing touch to our satisfaction. There is freedom on both sides; the street and the ramparts become our property. We take possession of the latter at once, by going out through our door upon the walk, four feet broad, which runs along the top of the ramparts, interrupted by a succession of flights of grassy steps,

from the portcullis to the gate of the abbey. On
the other side of it is a wall breast-high, against
which we lean and look out on the strange scene
around us. The barren rippled sand stretches
away for some miles to the low belt of hills en-
circling it, now covered with a purplish haze. A
few winding streams of water, which look like
paths, cross the plain, with here and there a
shallow pool, ankle deep, lying in the hollows,
where it was left by the last tide. Beneath us
a plumb-line would fall down straight for some
two hundred feet, to the foundation of granite
rocks on which the wall is built. At this hour
groups of women and children are scattered
over the sands, seeking shell-fish in the shallow
pools, and filling the air with their clear shrill
cries. Nearer at hand, there is a faint chirping
of birds, and we can catch the sound of voices
and footsteps in the abbey above us, as a party of visitors passes through its echoing halls
and galleries. But there is no noise of horses or
wheels, no steamers or railway engines with
their harsh whistle. All is perfect tranquillity
and repose in the summer sunshine, and the
air that just breathes upon us delicately from
the sea, which shines one single line of glistening light on the horizon, is deliciously pure and
fresh.

All the figures on the sand stand out with
singular distinctness, and cast clear shadows,
which seem to dog them as they pace along.
Yonder are three priests, probably three of

the monks whose home is in the abbey, coming slowly towards the town gate, in their black
robes and peaked hats. A fisherman, in a long
buff dress of some kind, with part of it drawn
over his head, is stepping busily out seaward. A
cart comes carefully over the plain with a load
of peasants, whose laughter rings up to us. A
few sea-gulls are flying by; we see them first by
their shadows flitting below them as rapidly as
they. Most of the afternoon we spend upon the
ramparts, paying a visit now and then to the
arch over the portcullis to watch the business
going on in the inns below.

At four o'clock, when the rush of pilgrims
and tourists is over, we present ourselves at
the abbey gate. It stands half-way up a broad
staircase, under a vaulted roof, with an obscure
and gloomy twilight falling upon it from some
opening above. Two immense folding doors of
massive wood, studded with nails, confront us,
closed as if no mortal hand could open them.
As we ring a bell, a small door, too low for us
to enter without stooping, swings back, and we
continue to ascend the staircase till we reach a
large vestibule or hall, and find in it two or three
stalls, precisely like those in a modern bazaar,
containing a variety of souvenirs of Mont St.
Michel. The stalls are presided over by a black-
robed brother of the monastery, who solemnly
summons a guide, and we are handed over to
him, having the good fortune to have the place
shown to us alone, unaccompanied by a troop of

visitors. The guide is a bright, handsome boy of eighteen, who is quickly lured away from his formal routine of duty, and becomes eager to converse with us, grieving, with a very genuine and ingenuous sorrow, over us when we tell him, in answer to his inquiry, that we are Protestants as well as Englishwomen. "What a pity! What a pity!" he exclaims, the tears springing to his bright young eyes; "I must pray much for you." It is evident that he regards us with as great a compassion as if we were sunk in deep and degrading superstition.

The lower part of the Monument, as the massive pile of buildings is called by the inhabitants, consists of a strongly fortified citadel, containing many mysterious passages and vaults, with great halls and saloons of Gothic architecture. The vestibule was partly hollowed out of the rock in 1117, and during the feudal ages served as guard-house and servants' hall. Two staircases, formed in the thickness of the wall, lead to a magnificent saloon above, *la salle de chevaliers*, divided into four aisles by three rows of pillars, with finely sculptured capitals. Above this saloon are the cloisters, the most beautiful portion of the building; the whole of this part of the Monument is named the "Marvel," for its wonderful strength and magnificence. These cloisters are truly a marvel of architecture. They stand almost on the summit of the rock, surrounding a square court, open to the blue sky, and that alone, with no other object visible,

except here and there, where one of the pointed
archways is left open to form a frame to the won-
drous picture of sea and sand and distant hills,
which seem all unreal and dream-like. There
are two hundred and twenty columns, standing in three close ranks, with arches intersect-
ing one another and resting upon thin granite
pillars, some of which are highly polished. The
spandrils of the arches are filled up with exqui-
sitely designed ornaments of leaves, fruit, and
flowers, each one different, and wrought in soft
white limestone which has kept a wonderful
clearness and sharpness of outline. The silence
up here is supreme; one feels lifted up far above
all the stir and tumult of the busy world, even
of the little town beneath, with its single street
and small group of houses, which, compared
with this still solitude, seems a very Babel of
confusion and noise.

Descending from the cloisters we enter the
church, where our devout young guide dis-
plays to us some remarkable relics, and still
more remarkable and grotesque bas-reliefs.
Everywhere, even here, are traces of the use the
Monument was put to from the edict of the sup-
pression of monasteries in 1790 until nine years
ago, when the late Emperor Napoleon restored
it to the bishopric of Avranches and Coutances.
It was used as a prison, and the nave of the
church itself was divided into three storeys,
which were turned into workshops for the pris-
oners, whilst the walls, with their sculptures

and bas-reliefs and frescoes, were thickly white-washed. Beneath the nave of the church lies an immense saloon, gloomy and vaulted, which was the ancient cemetery of the monks. In the midst of this darksome place are found the entrances to some *oubliettes*, places of oblivion, where persons condemned to be buried alive were left to their horrible fate. At the end of this saloon are also the entrances to several flights of steps, which descend to unknown vaults and caves in the rock, but they have not lately been explored, and are fallen into ruins.

A very singular crypt lies below the choir of the church. It contains a cluster of enormous round columns, set very closely together, to the number of twenty. The whole place is subterranean, of vast proportions, and of excessive gloom, being lighted only by a feeble lamp burning before a figure of the Virgin, which is placed in the midst of the clusters of pillars.

We are conducted through a damp and sombre gallery, with a faint streak of daylight here and there making the road practicable, to see the dungeons and the miserable black holes where, in the good old times, distinguished offenders were imprisoned. Here was a famous cage for such eminent persons, made of thick beams set three inches apart. One of the last occupants was an unfortunate German writer, Dubourg, who had offended the tyrant Louis XIV, and who passed long years in it, occupying himself with carving the beams with a nail. The unhappy man is said to have perished miserably, being completely paralysed in his limbs by the cold and damp, and disabled from defending himself against the rats that invaded his horrible cage.

We are glad to get out of these gloomy galleries, after watching some men wind provisions up into the monastery by treading an enormous wooden wheel, and so drawing them along an almost perpendicular shoot. There are a few more turrets and platforms to visit, and then we escape from the dark and heavy place into the open day and bright sunshine of the outer air. We are in time to have a stroll round the rock before the sun sets. It is not more than three quarters of a mile, and the only attraction is to get a little way from the mount to see how high it stands above us. There is a curious noise under our feet, which puzzles us at first; and knowing that there are said to be quicksands about, it has the effect of making us hurry back to the solid rock under the wall. As we tread upon the sand, a low, indistinct sound—you might call it a sigh or a squeak, according to your temperament and frame of mind—follows each step. But after all we discover that it is nothing more than the air that has been shut in under the sand by the last tide, which is set free by the pressure of our feet.

The sun is setting as we reach the gate again, and half the population are gathered about it with sunburnt and weather-beaten faces, mostly

calm and unexcited, as of people who know nothing of the turmoil and strife of modern times,
and whose chief care is to seek their daily food
upon the sands surrounding their rock. After we
have had dinner in the inn-parlour, as there are
other guests to be served and no room for us,
chairs are placed out in the street near the door;
and we sit there awhile, wondering if we can be
in the same hemisphere that contains London
and Paris. Before us rises the black wall of the
ramparts; a narrow strip of sky passes over our
heads, with stars beginning to twinkle all along
it; the dark gateway, with its strange, grotesque
figures coming through it homewards, stands
close by; and just beside us is the inn-kitchen,
with its open hearth and crackling fire of sticks;
its gipsy-looking landlady cooking delicious om-
elettes and fried fish over it; a group of solemn-
looking men eating their supper in silence, their
brown faces lit up by a bright oil lamp; and the
same clear light falling upon the curly head of
a little child, who is sleeping soundly on a bed
in a low recess, with scarlet curtains before it,
very like one of the berths onboard the steamer
which brought us to St. Malo.

At nine o'clock our landlord conducts us,
with a lantern to guide our steps, along the narrow street, telling us as much of his own history as he can get in by the way, and he leaves
us in unshared possession of our house on the
ramparts. We can hear from our beds the cease-
less rustling of the poplar leaves, and the far-off

wail of a sea-gull; and are conscious of nothing else, until suddenly our eyes open to see a crimson ball of fire rising out of the distant sea line, and flooding the brown, barren plain with a ruddy bright glare which picks out every ripple on the sand, and makes the whole landscape stretched before our eyes wild and weird even in the morning light. For a minute we fancy we are dreaming of the desert, and of sunrise across it; but this is no dream. The sum is rising over the sands round the Mont St. Michel; and one of our long cherished dreams has been realised.

A pleasant morning we spend in loitering about the ramparts, exploring every nook and corner of the rock, and talking with the natives, who are at leisure until the hour when the visitors begin to come. Before the morning has worn away we seem to know everybody, and to be known by them. We have found out the respectable people and the discreditable people; we have watched the troop of boys and girls mounting the flights of steps leading to the monastery, as they carry their water-jars and pails to fill them at the cistern, which is open to them once a day; we have discovered a black-faced sheep, tethered on a little platform of a garden levelled on the rock; visited the town church, and heard that the inhabitants, very like those of larger places, shirk the services, and prefer the short low mass of the monastery to the long, high mass of their parish church; we have copied an inscription over a grave in the burial ground:—"I was like you; you will be like me;" we have been sitting upon the grassy steps in the shade, and watched the lizards run about the wall; and we have made out every tower and half-moon and bastion along the fortifications.

All this we have done, yet the one thing we came for we have not seen, and cannot see, unless we stay here a whole week. The tide which pours in over the level sands, and advances against the mount like a horse at full gallop, and dashes so fiercely against its rocks and walls as sometimes to break into the guard-house in the outer court, does so only at springtides, and now we are precisely at dead water, when the sea lies peacefully off yonder in the distance, like a sleeping lamb. There is no help for it. We feel as if we knew everything that could ever happen in this out-of-the-world spot; all its resources are known to us, there is not a spot left to be explored. To stay a week here, without books, newspapers, or work, would be impossible. We promise ourselves to come again some time when the tide will be high; and we bid farewell to the Mont St. Michel, with some of the regret one feels in quitting an old familiar place. When we are miles away, we look back for the last time and see the Monument standing out, a miniature rock in a miniature bay, but still distinct and clear, as a place standing alone, and set upon a hill.

Made in the USA
Monee, IL
24 February 2022

91739621R10031